The
Buried
Moon

For Holly and Bruce,
and with thanks to the Boys and Girls in Black Street

Copyright © 1991 by Amanda Walsh
First American edition 1991
Originally published in Australia in 1991 by Houghton Mifflin Australia Pty Ltd.

Printed in Hong Kong

10 9 8 7 6 5 4 3 2 1

CIP information is available from the U.S. Library of Congress.

Designed by Lynne Tracey
Typeset in Goudy Bold by Bookset, Melbourne

The
Buried
Moon

Amanda Walsh

Houghton Mifflin Company
Boston 1991

A long time ago, it was certain death to walk through the Marshlands after dark. Only when the Moon was shining brightly could a traveler hope for a safe journey through the treacherous bogs that slithered and gurgled all around.

For on nights when the Moon did not appear, and it was pitch-dark, out would come the Hidden Folk who fear light — Bogles, Dead Things and Night Demons — to frighten travelers and lead them astray. Many a poor person going home in the darkness had been tricked into quicksand or mudpools by these Horrors.

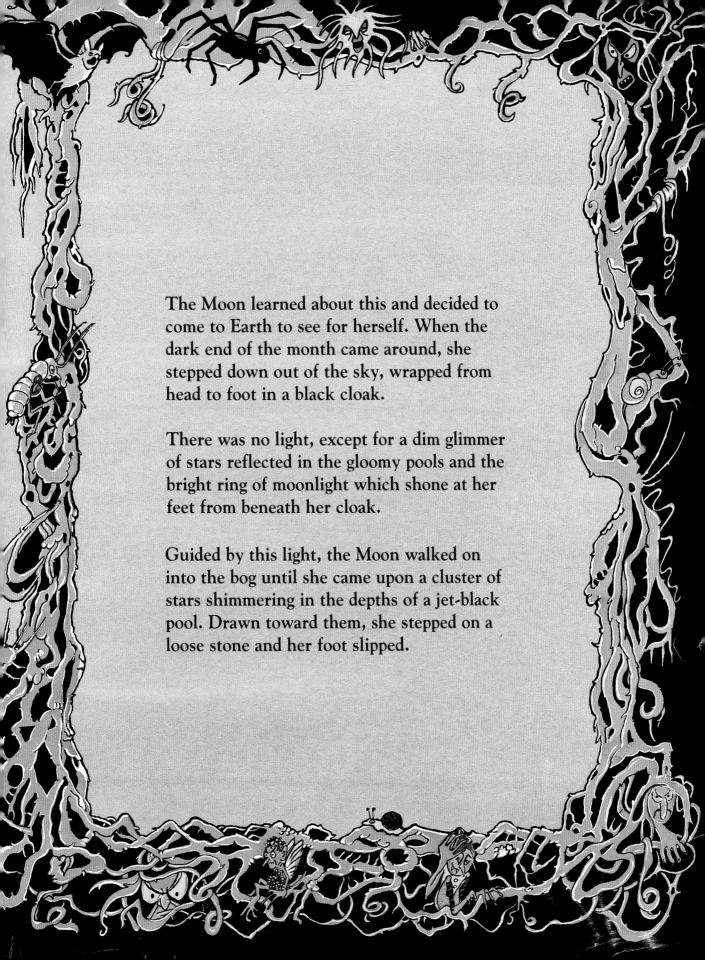

The Moon learned about this and decided to
come to Earth to see for herself. When the
dark end of the month came around, she
stepped down out of the sky, wrapped from
head to foot in a black cloak.

There was no light, except for a dim glimmer
of stars reflected in the gloomy pools and the
bright ring of moonlight which shone at her
feet from beneath her cloak.

Guided by this light, the Moon walked on
into the bog until she came upon a cluster of
stars shimmering in the depths of a jet-black
pool. Drawn toward them, she stepped on a
loose stone and her foot slipped.

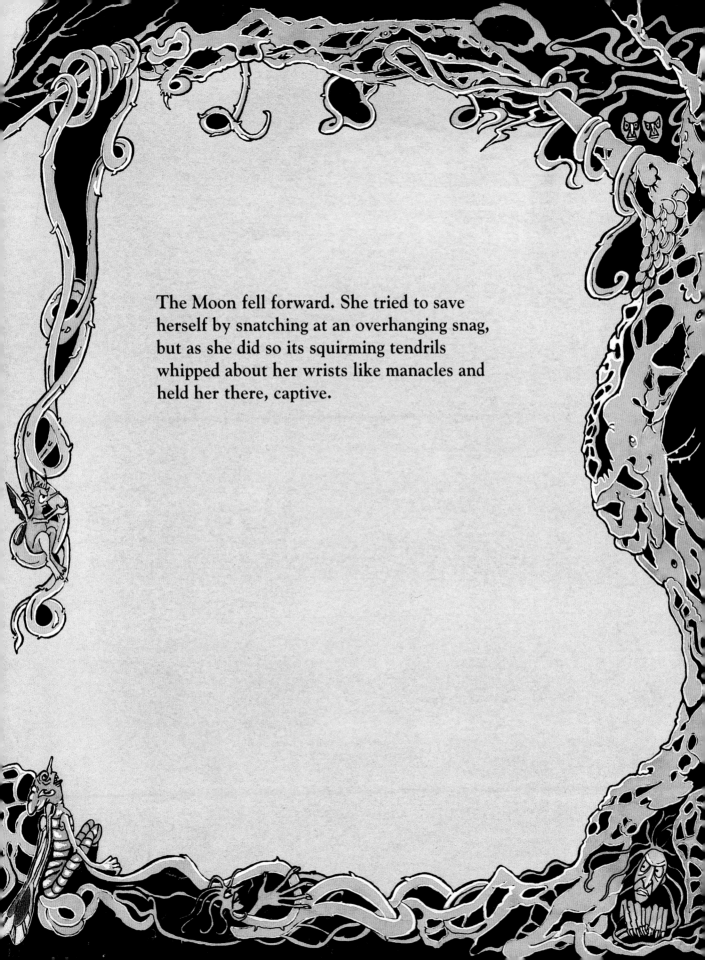

The Moon fell forward. She tried to save
herself by snatching at an overhanging snag,
but as she did so its squirming tendrils
whipped about her wrists like manacles and
held her there, captive.

The Moon stood shivering in the darkness. Then, far away in the mist, she heard a voice calling for help. She listened. The cry came nearer, and she heard footsteps, halting and stumbling. At last, by the dim light of the stars, she glimpsed the pale, frightened face of a man who had lost his way and was floundering on through the bog. He had seen the gleam of light coming from the captive Moon, and was making his way toward it.

The man drew closer, and the Moon realized
that her light was luring him to his death. She
doubled her efforts to free herself.

As the Moon struggled, the hood of her cloak fell back and revealed her dazzling silver hair. Immediately, the muddy pools and all the gnarled, twisted roots and snags were flooded with light, making the bog as clear as day.

In the sudden brightness, the terrified traveler could see the Things all around him as they scurried back to their holes for safety. He could now see his way home too, and he hurried off through the moonlit Marshlands.

The Moon sank exhausted into the mud at the
foot of the snag. But her head fell forward and
the cloak once more covered her brightly shining
hair. The bog was dark again.

In one swoop, the loathsome Things appeared
once more, writhing and wriggling out from the
depths of their dank black hiding-places. The
Moon heard their whispering, which grew louder
and louder as they swarmed about on the marshes.

The Dead Things and the crawling Horrors
gathered around the Moon, snarling and
scratching and taunting her.

"Hell roast thee, meddlesome creature!"
cried an ugly old Witch-thing. "You'll not
be spoiling any more of my brews!"

"Away with you!" shrieked the Bogle-bodies.
"If it were not for you, we'd have this place
to ourselves."

They clamored and screeched, raising a horrible din against the Moon, until their ugly, cracked voices joined with the very gurgles of the bog in a celebration of hate.

Near dawn, the Things were still hissing and clawing at one another over the best way to get rid of the Moon. The quickest way now was surely to bury her. So they clutched at their prisoner with bony fingers, pushing her down into the black slime at the foot of the snag. The Bogle-bodies ran to fetch a great stone to place over her, and the Witch-thing ordered two will-o'-the-wisps to keep watch over the Moon's grave.

Pleased with their night's work, the Horrors crept, chuckling, back into their dark holes.

Many days passed, and the time of the New
Moon, so eagerly awaited by the marsh
dwellers, finally arrived. But the twilight
brought no Moon. The nights remained
pitch-black, and no traveler was safe.

Even the Wise Old Woman of the village did
not know why the Moon had forsaken them.

More nights went by and still no Moon appeared. Then one evening, at the local inn, a man from the other side of the Marshlands began to tell a strange story.

He told of how he had become lost in the bogs one night, and had blundered onward with all kinds of Horrors chasing after him. He had been saved at the last moment by a miraculous light that burst from a pool of black water, showing him the way to go.

On hearing this, some of the marsh dwellers
hurried off to consult the Wise Old Woman
again. For many minutes she gazed into her
magic mirror. At last she announced:
"Although it is dark, for there is no Moon to
conjure by, I can now tell you how to find
her."

And she gave each of them a twig of witch
hazel to guard against harm, saying, "Go
into the marshes and search for a coffin, and
a cross, and a candle. There you will find
the Moon, if you are lucky!"

The following night, the marsh dwellers
crept silently into the bogland. The weirdest
whispers hissed past their ears, while cold
wet hands with bony fingers plucked at their
lucky charms.

And then they saw it — the grotesque stone!
Indeed, it did look just like a coffin. And
there, too, was the cross formed out of the
branches of a snag, and a will-o'-the-wisp
flickering and gleaming like a small candle.

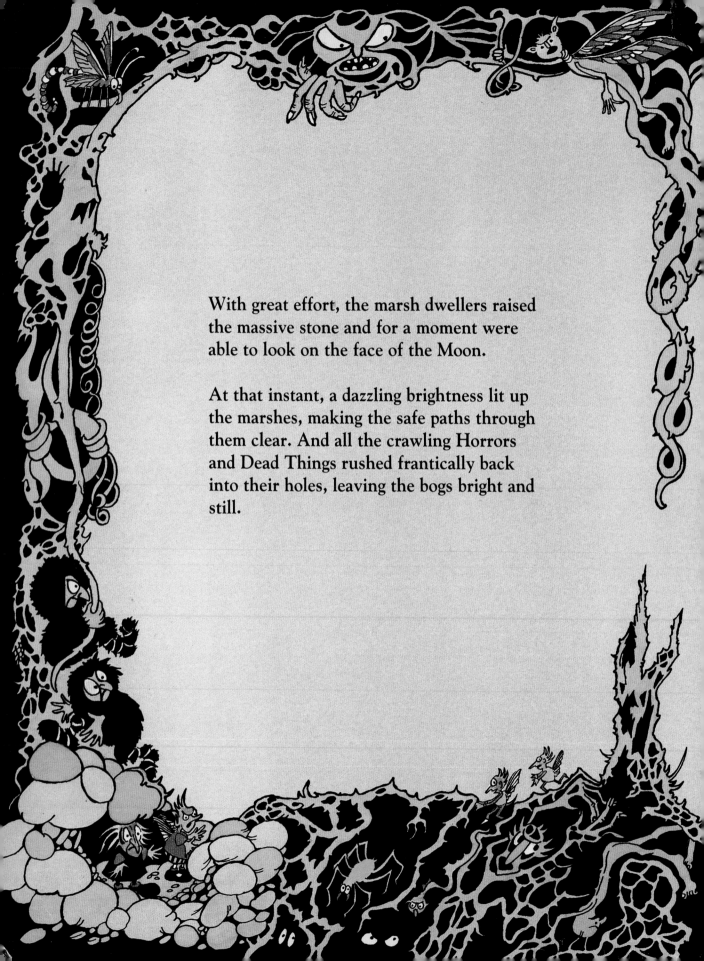

With great effort, the marsh dwellers raised the massive stone and for a moment were able to look on the face of the Moon.

At that instant, a dazzling brightness lit up the marshes, making the safe paths through them clear. And all the crawling Horrors and Dead Things rushed frantically back into their holes, leaving the bogs bright and still.

Looking up, the rescuers could see the Full Moon
sailing in the sky, lighting their way home.